Lillibutt's Big Adventure

In Medieval times there were three great pilgrimages that people would walk for religious reasons – Rome, Jerusalem, and Santiago de Compostela in Spain. People still walk them today, 1000 years later and in 2010 almost 300,000 people walked El Camino de Santiago/ The Way of St James.

Tradition says that Santiago is the burial place of St James the Apostle. Legend has it that after he died his body was transported in a stone boat. He was washed ashore after a great storm and found covered in scallops. He was then buried in a field nearby. Later, a mighty cathedral was built over his tomb. Since then the scallop shell has been the symbol of the Camino and worn by all pilgrims. They also carry a passport, a credencial, which is stamped at each stop. On completing they earn a compostela, a certificate of accomplishment in Latin. El Camino follows the route of the Milky Way, which is said to be formed by the dust kicked up by pilgrims, and compostela means 'field of stars'.

In 2009 Maris O'Rourke walked the Camino. On the way she met a charming, and obviously lonely, little pig. She couldn't take the pig with her but she thought that one day someone should …

The pathways that lead from France to Santiago de Compostela

Lillibutt's Big Adventure

By Maris O'Rourke

Illustrated by Claudia Pond Eyley

DUCK CREEK PRESS

There was once a little pig called Lillibutt who lived by the Pyrenees –

the mountains that lie between France and Spain.

Lillibutt was lonely.

    Lillibutt was bored.

        Lillibutt longed for an adventure.

Every day Lillibutt saw people walking by.

She wondered where they were going.

She would run eagerly to the fence
        wriggle her fat little body,
    wiggle her curly little tail,
shine her bright little eyes and call

'Take me, take me …
oh please take me with you.'

But no-one ever did.

One day a young girl stopped.

'Hello, I'm Zoë. What's your name?'

'I'm Lillibutt. Take me, take me … oh please take me with you!'

Zoë smiled.

'But I am walking the Camino. It is a very, very long way. It is very, very difficult.

You will have to climb mountains.

You will be hot.

You will be cold.

You will be wet.

You will be hungry.

You will be thirsty.

Your feet will hurt.

We will walk in silence.

Are you really sure you want to come?'

'I am.

I'm lonely.

I'm bored.

I've been stuck in this pen all my life.

I want an adventure!'

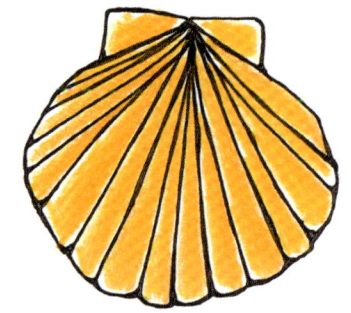

'Ok then, come with me.' Zoë said.

'We will walk together to Santiago de Compostela on paths pilgrims have trod for over a thousand years.'

And she hung a scallop shell around Lillibutt's neck.

Zoë and Lillibutt climbed over the Pyrenees Mountains into Spain.

Lillibutt's feet hurt.

'Are we nearly there?'
'No,' said Zoë.

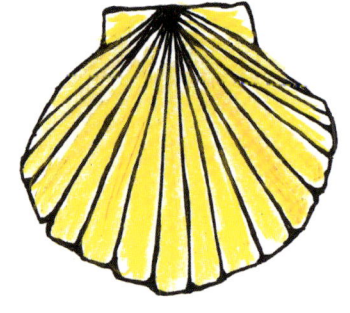

All day every day they walked.

They walked across the Basque region.

Lillibutt was tired.

'Are we nearly there?'

'No,' said Zoë.

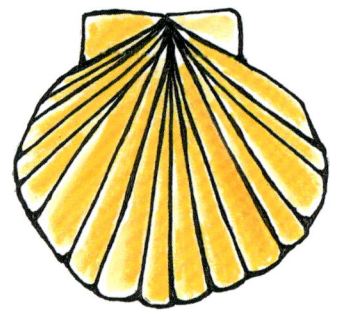

All day every day they walked and walked.

They walked through the vineyards of La Rioja.

Lillibutt was hot.

'Are we nearly there?'

'No,' said Zoë.

On the way they slept under the stars and Zoë named the great constellations as they wheeled across the sky.

All day every day they walked and walked and walked.

They walked across the high meseta and dry plains of Castilla y Leon.

Lillibutt was thirsty.

'Are we nearly there?'
'No,' said Zoë.

All day every day they walked and walked and walked and walked.

They walked past churches and convents and monasteries.

Lillibutt was getting thinner.

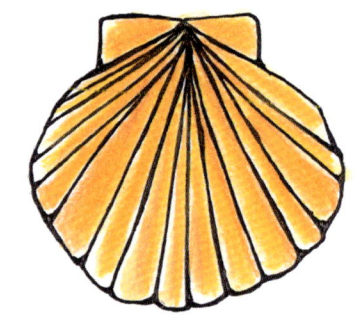

'Are we nearly there?'

'No,' said Zoë.

All day every day they walked and walked and walked and walked and walked.

They climbed the craggy, rocky mountains of Galicia.

Lillibutt was cold.

'Are we nearly there?'
'No,' said Zoë.

Finally, after 40 days and 40 nights
they came to the walls of
Santiago de Compostela.

'Are we nearly there?'
'Yes,' said Zoe. 'We're there!'

Word of their long pilgrimage
had spread far and wide.

Crowds gathered to cheer and cheer and cheer
    and clap and clap and clap
        and wave and wave and wave
        and sing and sing and sing
        as they walked in.

Lillibutt forgot her sore feet.

She forgot all about being

hot,

    cold,

        wet,

            hungry,

                thirsty

                    and tired

as she ran to the great Cathedral.

Zoë turned to Lillibutt.

'So … shall we find another adventure?'

Lillibutt
      wriggled her not-so-fat little body,
    wiggled her ever-so-curly little tail,
shone her now-even-brighter little eyes

and said, 'Oh yes please!'

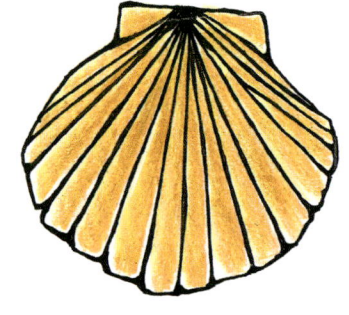

DUCK CREEK PRESS

An imprint of David Ling Publishing Limited
PO Box 34 601 Birkenhead
Auckland 0746 New Zealand
www.davidling.co.nz

Hardback ISBN 978-1-877378-58-4
Paperback ISBN 978-1-877378-59-1

First Published 2012

© 2012 Maris O'Rourke and Claudia Pond Eyley

This book is copyright. Apart from any fair dealing for the purpose of private study, research, criticism, or review as permitted under the Copyright Act, no part may be reproduced by any process without the prior written permission of the Publisher.

Typeset by Express Communications Limited
Printed in China

Maris O'Rourke is a former Secretary for Education for New Zealand and the first Director of Education for The World Bank. She has worked in, or on, education in up to 50 developing countries. Like Lillibutt, she enjoys walking and adventure. She is also an accomplished poet and in the last three years has published in a range of poetry journals and been winner or runner-up in a number of poetry competitions. She lives and works in Mt Eden, Auckland. This is her first children's book.

Visual artist, painter, printmaker, film director, Claudia Pond Eyley was born in Matamata, New Zealand and attended schools in Montreal, Canada and New York. She returned to New Zealand to attend the School of Fine Arts at the University of Auckland in the mid 1960s and continues to practise from her studio in Mt Eden, Auckland. The gorgeous models for Lillibutt live at the Auckland Zoo and do go for 'guided' walks every day with their keepers.
www.claudiapondeyley.com